Joseph C. Stiles

Capt. Thomas E. King

Or, a word to the army and the country

Joseph C. Stiles

Capt. Thomas E. King
Or, a word to the army and the country

ISBN/EAN: 9783337427634

Printed in Europe, USA, Canada, Australia, Japan

Cover: Foto ©Andreas Hilbeck / pixelio.de

More available books at **www.hansebooks.com**

CAPT. THOMAS E. KING;

OR,

A WORD TO THE ARMY AND THE COUNTRY.

BY REV. JOSEPH C. STILES, D. D.

CHARLESTON, S. C.:
The South Carolina Tract Society.
1864.

ATLANTA, GEORGIA:
Franklin Printing House.
J. J. TOON & CO., PROPRIETORS.

CAPT. THOS. E. KING.

On the 19th day of September, 1863, the Confederate Army, under General Bragg, and the Federal forces, under Gen. Rosecrans, were drawn up in line of battle on Chickamauga creek. Brig. Gen. Preston Smith, whose scars testified to his gallantry in the past, and whose life-blood upon the battle-field closed his heroic service of his country that very day, it was well known was about to enter upon the responsibilities of a momentous conflict with an *inadequate* staff. All hearts and eyes are now addressed to the front. A mounted stranger, in military dress, is seen beside the General; he may be a casual acquaintance who will presently retire.— He accompanies the commanding General from one point to another; still he

may only seek friendly conference until
the battle commences.   The cannon is
booming, the musketry is rattling; but
the stranger has not disappeared.   See!
he rides rapidly here and there, bearing
the General's orders to his colonels,
along the line.   The secret is revealed.
He has come to share the perils of the
day, and to serve the General and his
brigade through all the vicissitudes of
the deadly conflict.   But how different
the moral position of the parties!   On
the one hand, the General and his brigade are under the most solemn legal obligation, every man of them, to brave
all the dangers of the impending battle:
an obligation the violation of which
would perpetrate a crime of crimson hue,
and incur a penalty severe unto blood.
On the other, the unknown soldier sus-
tains no such obligation, and risks nothing by declining to take part in the conflict.   Why then should he peril his very
life, and hazard all he holds dear on

earth, by throwing himself between the enemy and his every shot and shell aimed at the brigade? Ah! how impressively, if silently, he exclaims, "I love my country! Her cause is just! Invaded by a powerful and malignant foe, my fortune, strength and life, all, all are hers, cheerfully hers!" Amidst the roar of cannon, whistle of shells, fall of men, and all the stunning din of battle, all day long, with a buoyant heart, bright countenance, animated tone and martial port, he bears commands, leads regiments and encourages troops. Thus, all day long, with admirable eloquence he expounds the loud calls of patriotism when our country is invaded, and the radiant nobility of courage when adverse power presses fearfully. Through all the varying issues of that memorable day, the ever gallant conduct of the volunteer soldier, how it must have inspired the patriotic devotion of the combatants!--infixing upon taste many a vivid impression of the exquisite beauty of patriot heroism—inscribing upon many a conscience that only harbinger of national independence, the moral conviction, "*Every man should be a hero when his country's liberty is imperilled.*" Study all its influence, present and ultimate, and who can tell what a valuable work, even towards national deliverance, may be wrought by one day's gallant volunteer fighting by an unknown soldier on the common battle ground of our country's liberty, especially if sealed with his blood?

The responsibilities of the day are over, the enemy have been driven for miles, the soldier has laid by his musket, the army is at rest. Our nameless officer, without a solitary acquaintance in the brigade, sits down to commune with a friend whose intimate fellowship, especially in anxious hours, he has long since learned to appreciate. In solitude, with a calm, firm hand, he pencilled in his note book the following record : "Saturday, 19th, 5 P. M.   Have seen the enemy once more.   The roar of the cannon and the rattle of the musketry bringing vividly to mind the memorable 21st of July, 1861 ; from which time I have been out of service.   Brig. Gen. Preston Smith gave me position on his staff.   Through the mercies of a kind Providence, who has shielded me with His wings, and covered me, I have been preserved without a wound, amidst the hundreds wounded around me, and the thousands of shot and shell which sung the requiem of our dead boys.   Thank God who gave me strength, I feel that so far as I am concerned I have done my duty.   All is quiet along the lines.   The result I do not yet know.   Sharp shoot ers are pegging away, but no brigade is engaged.   My loving wife and my little boys, I know, pray for me."

Ah! how little did he know his most solemn need of their wrestling interces- sions at that very hour.   The brigade is startled, and all is a-stir. The command from Gen. Polk has been delivered, "Forward! and drive the enemy from his strong position on the heights across the creek." The troops are in motion, the brave General is in front, our gallant volunteer by his side. They charge the enemy; a volley is delivered by the retreating foe. Not an officer escapes; all are shot to the ground. Capt. Donelson fell dead; Gen. Smith died in half an hour; and in one hour more the soul of our unknown hero joined him in the Spirit land. A few days after the battle, the bodies of these brave men were brought from the field under military escort. Our Volunteer Soldier, was buried in his own town—it is hardly proper to say with military honors, for the community, in mass, bond and free, arose to receive the remains of the man they loved and honored, and most devoutly laid them away in the home prepared for all living.

Doubtless when the brigade had obeyed the Lieutenant General's command and driven the enemy from his fortified heights, and wreaked their vengeance on his slaughtered multitudes, and were now at rest once more, deeply, *deeply* did the soldiers mourn the death of their brave, beloved commander, who had led them to victory in almost half the States of the Confederacy. And surely their thoughts must have rushed to the unknown departed. How brief, how brilliant his career! He was seen for the first time in the morning; he fights by their side throughout the day; he is seen no more at night. How seasonable, how generous his visit! He came to fill an important vacancy; he discharged its perilous duties to universal admiration. Sword in hand from first to last, with heroic gallantry he presses through every successive obligation of the day, and mingles his heart's blood with their General's at night. We need no witness to

testify that when the fighting was over,
the victory won, and all was quiet, the
strange and striking history of the unknown must have starved in the bosom
of many a private in that brigade some
such hearty enquiries as these : " Who
was this volunteer Captain who seemed,
in the morning to be dropped upon us
like an angel to fight the battle of the
day, and who went home to heaven at
even-tide when his work was done?—
What was his name, and what his military connection ?   Where did he abide,
and what was his calling in life ?   What
style of man was he, and what impelled
him to seek his glorious end in our ranks ?
Whatever incipient interest in the stranger may have been awakened by the intimate and eventful interweaving of his
personal history with theirs for the space
of a day, all that interest will be pro-
foundly augmented by an honest answer
to the personal enquiries so naturally
suggested.

The volunteer aid who fought and fell by the side of Gen. Preston Smith, at the battle of Chickamauga, near the close of the day and battle of the 19th of September, was CAPT. THOMAS E. KING, son of BARRINGTON KING, Esq., both of Roswell, Cobb County, Georgia.

Capt. King possessed a well balanced character, a good education, quick and excellent judgment, great energy and remarkable business capacity ; a rare combination of gentleness and firmness.— Few men were so pure, simple and modest; and fewer still, endued with such universal, captivating benevolence. He seemed to go through life with a radiant smile upon his face, and rarely met a human being without a gush of kindness. Pre-eminently genial, he fell into animated sympathy with his companion upon sight; yet never lacked dignity or decision when circumstances called .for either. To the day of his death profound veneration for his father, and ten-

derness for his mother, were not exhib-
ited by word and act only, but invaria-
bly found touching expression in the very
tones of his voice. 'Twas a simple, beautiful testimony to the winning loveliness
of his fraternal affection that the five
younger children should have uniformly
addressed him by the tender appellation
of 'Brother,' while they always distin-
guished their three elder and excellent
brethren by prefixing this generic address to their respective names. Of his
conjugal and parental tenderness we will
not speak. To say that he ardently
loved his family, kindred and friends,
and shared the reciprocal affection of all,
leaves a larger truth untold. The fact
is, he loved every child of Adam, rich
and poor, and was always the most pop-
ular man in the community, both with
the bond and the free. Naturally unob-
trusive, he died Mayor of the town and
Commander of the Post. No man was
so familiarly approached for a favor by

the affluent or the indigent; yet no man
could so readily subdue an insurgent
population by suasion or by ——
While every manly and —— ——
composed the basis —— character,
prompt and cheerful —— with the
dependent classes of society, probably
constituted his most distinguishing trait.
Many a time has his hand distributed
enlarged benefactions to the indigent, of
which the world never heard. The poor
as well as the rich, the bond as well as
the free, broke their hearts around
his grave, and now fill the public ear
with the celebration of his virtues, the
memory of his kindnesses, their appreciation of his value, and the expressions
of their grief. The servant of one neigh-
bor, near at hand, dressed her cake at
thicker and sent it to the Captain's
breakfast table on the morning of his departure for the army; another, at a
distance, sent "Many howdyes to Miss
Tom" on the day of his death. —— a

triumphant endorsement of the beautiful
symmetry of his character, the unsullied
rectitude of his life, that, though so uniformly successful in all his social, business and military relations, he should
have excited so little envy, and that the
few unprincipled and selfish men who
did harbor unkindness towards him rarely expressed it, well knowing in their
shrewdness that universal admiration of
his virtues would very soon have crushed
both them and their opposition.

In sketching the character of our departed soldier in this critical hour of
our country's history, it is seasonable to
remark, if by nature his generic charac-
teristic was *benevolence*, by providence
and grace its specific developments were
patriotism and *piety*.

I. PATRIOTISM.—The spirit he breath-
ed and the principles of his conduct are
clearly indicated by the following extracts from his private correspondence
and his army journal, recorded without

comment in the order in which he penn-
ed them :

"Milledgeville, Jan. 18th, 1861.—
Hurrah! hurrah! hurrah! hurrah! hurrah! One for each sovereign State and
independent Sovereignty. It was to-day
'Resolved that Georgia has a right and
should secede from the Union;' passed
at 4 o'clock P. M. by 35 majority. Our
cannon are proclaiming it to the world."
"Atlanta, May 31st, 1861.—To-day we
were mustered into the volunteer service
of the Confederate States." "June 1st.—
Rose at 4 o'clock this morning; the hour
I have fixed for regular rising during the
war." "June 11th.—Though naturally
you feel ' *desolate* and *lonely*,' I thank my
God that you have been enabled to 'give
me up in so noble a cause." "Winchester,
Va., June 28.—I find myself on ground hal-
lowed by associations with the noble Vir-
ginian, George Washington. Our camp
is a quarter of a mile from the house.
Perhaps we are on the very spot where

his troops encamped 101 years ago.
At any rate we are on a similar mission;
for as he was sent to drive back the in-
vader, so are we; and our prayer is that
his God may be our God, and crown us
too with victory. I never was in better
health, and I might say spirits, but for
the yearning of my heart for *home* and
friends. I will only have to fight the
harder for a forced peace, when I have
the opportunity. For one, I did not
come here for the sake of glory and re-
nown. I came to secure the blessings of
peace and prosperity to ourselves and
our children. This was, and is what I
desire, and my voice would go forth in
songs of grateful, heartfelt thanksgivings
if the knife could be buried, and all
sounds of war quieted within our borders. But if, like fiends incarnate, nothing but *war, war* shall be their cry, why
then we say, let it come, and we will show
the fanatics what it is. to be *men* and to
stand up in fearless defence of our rights

and liberties; and again we say *let it come!* and God be with the right."

"Richmond, July 26th, (after the battle of Manassas.)— My Dear Father and darling Mother: Lin .... hearts have before this .... pride that your thanksgiving .... been most fervently poured out; and that your cup of blessing is now rich and overflowing. The 21st of July, a day pregnant with glorious .... events, has not its parallel in the annals of American history, if in the history of the world. If your ancestors boasted of the .... in revolutionary times, and justly too, so may you my dear parents, tell what your sons have done in these days. The battle of *Stone Bridge* introduces a new era in American history; for with it comes the acknowledged birth of a new nation. We began our march gloomy, disheartened and ripe for rebellion, until the gallant B......... each regiment, passing by, that this was no retreat

but a direct advance against the enemy.
Our hearts now grew light, our steps
buoyant.   We lay under a galling fire
for an hour, waiting orders.   About 11
o'clock Gen. Bartow ordered up our regiment to support GEN. BEE; but by the
time we reached him Bartow's (8th)
regiment was cut to pieces, and Bee's
brigade routed. · So they formed and
fell in behind us.   From this time until
3 o'clock the battle raged desperately,
and victory wavered.   About 3 Beaure-
gard told Bartow to take our flag and
lead on the two regiments, the 7th Georgia and 17th Virginia, and capture the
detachment of Sherman's battery which
was injuring our troops so much. Brave,
noble hearted man! he did it, but a bul-
let was sent to his heart and he fell dead.
We pressed on, however, nobly standing
our ground against fearful odds, and
drove back the gunners from a battery
of ten pieces.   Strong reinforcements
just then coming up enabled us to keep

the advantage. Here was the turning point of the day; for just after, the rout began. We were under the fire of near ten thousand men—regulars, Zouaves, and picked troops; the air actually seemed dense with flying bulllets. They grazed us on every side, and it is a miracle of miracles that every man of us was not mowed down. I was in the front rank, cheering on my men, when I was shot in the ancle, about 4 o'clock. I did not fall, but caught on my sword, and after a while, with help, hobbled to the rear. Our regiment might have been led on with more regularity and order. In fact it was nothing but a firm, dogged determination not to knuckle to a pesky Yankee, that made our boys hold their own. Shake hands with all the mourning ones around you for me. They must cease their mourning; for what offering can be more noble than theirs, sending their dear ones to be martyrs to our country's cause?"

Richmond, Aug. 20th.—" My leg is perfectly helpless, and sometimes very painful. Ordinarily it commences to distress me about 12 o'clock at night; from this time I begin to watch for the dawn. A splendid band, just now passing along the street -at the head of a company, puts my leg decidedly in the notion of stepping off to the time of the martial music. I try to keep off melancholy while prospecting my tedious convalescence, and only hope that the prophecies of the doctors may not be realized, but that at any rate by the middle of October I shall be able again to join my company. I am as anxious to be with them as they can possibly be to have me." Aug. 21st.—"Well, Father, it is just one month to-day since I had my bout with the Yankees. I have no occasion to regret it in any way, but would willingly go through all I have endured, and more, to have been with our troops in so glorious a fight as

Manassas. My heart beats with joy and yet is filled with sadness. I ~~before~~ five of us, brothers, all ~~assembled~~ in this room, in Richmond, ~~under the~~ hospitable roof of my ~~kind host~~, Mr. Pleasants. We ~~have shared~~ home comforts that we ~~may~~ stand up for our country's rights, for our own and our children's liberties. Providentially we all met here ~~this~~ morning, and, gathered around my ~~torn leg~~, renewed our vows to dedicate ~~ourselves~~ to our common cause, ~~the cause~~ of freedom ~~for our~~ precious Southern homes. ~~You, my father~~, have the honor of sending five ~~sons to battle~~ for your ~~country~~, and your heart must well up with ~~feelings of pride.~~ ~~Sept.~~ 2d—"I am ~~thinking~~ that my boys have gone forward ~~with the advance made~~ on the ~~Maryland shores.~~ I feel impressed with the ~~belief~~ that ~~momentous events overhang~~ us; ~~that~~ victory or annihilation ~~await our forces~~ on the ~~Po~~ tomac. I can only wield the ~~small but~~

powerful *engine of prayer* for our brave
soldiers and beloved land; and thank
God no Hessian fiend can deprive me of
this.   It chafes me no little to see the
result of their initiatory move against
our sea-coast defences, and my only hope
is that we may profit decidedly by it.—
We must expect reverses in the present
campaign; and should they overwhelm
our present forces I, for one, will not
be broken hearted, but will expect to
see our country rise, Phœnix like, from
her seeming ashes and show her malignant enemies an unbroken front, and hurl
them back from our polluted soil. I cannot look for annihilation to our forces;
I have too much confidence in the justness of our cause, and in the justice of
our God.   However protracted our
struggle, we must be victorious in the
end."

The *patriotic* spirit of the preceding
extracts was more gloriously developed
to the close of his life.   It was an entire

year before Capt. King laid aside his
crutches; he walked with a staff until he
died, and could not walk without it. He
took every step in pain, was thrown into pangs if his lame foot struck a pebble
and always to the ground if his staff did
not sustain him; he knew that he was a
cripple for life, and did not know that he
would outlive either the weakness or the
painfulness of his limb. It is a singular
fact, under all this physical discourage-
ment, that he should have gradually and
deliberately arrived at the conclusion to
consecrate his entire strength and service
to his country so long as the war should
last. To accomplish this purpose he employed himself for a long time in ar-
ranging his business, modifying his con-
nections w th society, making all proper
disposition of his domestic affairs, and
ultimately executed his will, and com-
mitted his children to the care of his
father. We are not surprised, therefore,
to find the following record in his war-

manual: "September 14th, 1863.—Left the dear ones at home again, having buckled on the sword to join the Army of Tennessee, under General Bragg, to strike another blow for independence and the freedom of Georgia from the polluting tread of the Abolitionists. My object is to join, as volunteer aid, the staff of Gen. Longstreet or Gen. Polk; this being the only service in the field where my help will avail anything."

It may be questioned whether the annals of the Confederacy furnish many exhibitions of the *love of country* more pure, sacred, or lofty, than that comprised in the last five days of Captain King's life, interpreted in the light of the previous record. We measure the force of an event by the resistance it overcomes. Test our soldier's patriotism by this rule. In the disabled state of his body his country had no right to call him out in her service; but he disdains all military exemption and marches out to

meet her enemies. He had a lovely
family, a large circle of appreciating
friends and relatives, and a buoyant,
cheerful heart to enjoy them; but he
surrenders all secular indulgence for
his country's service. He had a large
and lucrative occupation which needed
his constant, personal attention; but he
turns his back upon the attractive claims
of business and sallies forth to fight for
his country. He commanded the infant-
ry, cavalry and artillery recruited for
the home-defence of Roswell and its vi-
cinity; but, not anticipating an immedi-
ate raid, he obtains a furlough and seeks
the field where a desperate battle is
hourly expected. It is positively true
that he had no independent physical
ability, either to march on foot or to
mount a horse; but he could ride when
mounted, and therefore, refusing to avail
himself of his physical weakness, presses
on to meet the enemy. The influence
of a father's advice upon that son may

be inferred from the father's testimony that he could not recall a wish through life which that son had not anticipated; and yet he breaks through his father's incipient counsel, to go out and defend his country. His father said to him: "My son, you are not able to go." He responded, "Father, our State is invaded—our family is not represented on that battle field; I *must* go." It was a noble response: "Go, my son, and the Lord go with you." We must draw a veil over pleadings that were yet harder, to resist—those of his wife and children; yet even these he gently presses aside to serve his country. His clothes were not ready; but he felt that the battle was at hand, and could not wait for them. His servant's horse was stolen on the way; but he forbears to pursue the thief that he may not be too late at his post. He found Gen. Polk's staff well filled; but, undiscouraged, he seeks and finds his place on the staff of Brig. Gen.

Preston Smith, on the morning of the very day that he fought and bled.

Oh! the power of patriotic devotion in that young man's breast; what could withstand it? He felt that by a determined foe his country was sorely pressed just now, and must be as formidably overborne for a long time to come. He felt that every man should do all in his power for her defense. As for himself, he threw aside all legal exemption, all worldly indulgence, all business attractions, all honor of primary command at home, all bodily infirmity, all family solicitudes, and pressed rapidly to the very thickest of the fight. And was his patriotism tried, wearied, exhausted by all this? Far from it. He urged his way through all with a *cheerful will* which gathered strength from every sacrifice; a *devout consecration* which furnished courage for every emergency.—Exhausted indeed! when he was mounted for the last time, and going forth in

a few moments to his death, on a by-
stander remarking that his saddle did not
seem secure, with a bright countenance
and animated tone he exclaimed "That's
right, Doctor, see it well fastened; for
you know if I once get down I can't get
up again." Through all the duties and
perils of the day he went forth to his
death with so much of this same calm,
intrepid, heroic spirit; that, in perfect accordance with the public sentiment of
the brigade, one of the most distinguish-
ed officers of Gen. Polk's staff, on the
battle field, recorded with his own hand,
in Capt. King's war-manual, the following
tribute:—"*His gallantry upon the battle
field was conspicuous; and since this war
began, no nobler, braver, or truer heart
has been offered a sacrifice to the great
cause,*"—To this high encomium every
soldier of Gen. Smith's brigade who
served under him during his last
expedition, and every soldier who was
ever under his command in the Potomac

army, and every man who knew him
well at home, will delight to affix his
most hearty and solemn amen.

'Such a mind! What a lucid demon-
stration of the justice of our country's
cause, and of the duty of her every cit-
izen! What he was surely the
light of *truth*; what he felt was surely
the dictate of *rectitude*. What, then,
shall we think of those men in the Confederacy who act upon such opposite
principles! what shall we say to them?

Ye *speculators!* ye sordid money-ma
king *harpies* of the nation, who coolly
seek the very life-blood of the land to
feed your unhallowed lust of filthy lucre!
Look at him! He sacrificed covetousness
to patriotism and sought rather to serve
his country than to enrich himself.
ye and do likewise ere retribu-
tion overtake you at the hand patriot
who by privation, toil and blood,
shall have won a national liberty in
which they are deeply purposed that your

cold and cruel selfishness shall never, never have an honorable share. Ye heartless, worthless *exempts* in every corner of the land, who bribe the pliant surgeon to endorse your pretended disabilities! Look at him! You have twice the physical power to serve your country that he possessed; but in her extremity give her none of it. He first studied how he could best advance her interests, and then laid out in her service all the little strength he had. Go ye and follow his example; lest deep disgrace from an injured country settle upon you and your posterity for all time to come! Ye base and infamous *skulkers*, who hide a coward heart behind some fraction of a Nitre contract, or in some work or office that pays you well for the shelter it provides against the face of the enemy! Ye thousands of *furloughed sick, wounded and well*, scattered through the generous households of the people and your own homes, who by time and kind attention have regained your health and home refreshment, and are now every way fit for service, but, ignobly self-indulgent, still cling to the luxuries of the family when your struggling country calls you back to the hardships of the camp; whose entertainers grieve that their hospitalities have been spent upon such undeserving men, and, day and night, do now begrudge you that bed and board they would so gladly spread for the suffering faithful, returning from the battle field! And ye, *miserable stragglers*, who are sure to lose your regiment when an engagement is imminent! And ye, *pitiful cowards*, who are the scorn of the brave, because you are sure to become desperately ill when the line of battle is formed! And ye, *faint-hearted warriors*, who enter the battle but are sure to sneak out exhausted before you have fired a gun! Yes, all ye miserable skulkers of the country! look at him! look at *him!* When the noblest cause for which

man ever shed his blood was put in peril;
when the brightest flag the sun ever
shone upon was unfurled to the breeze;
when our country's liberties were actually placed upon trial by battle; did *he*
turn his back and abscond? Did he
seek an excuse to be absent from the
fray? Did he pretend to some physical
incapacity to stand at his post? Did he
content himself with luxurious indul-
gences at a distance when his country's
life was perilled on the battle field?—
No! never, never! Creation could not
keep him from his place in the ranks of
the faithful and the brave. Many and
strong were the powers that tried their
hand upon his patriotism; but they tried
in vain. Nor false pleas, nor sensual comforts, nor the cares of business, nor the
counsels of friends, nor the cries of kindred, nor a feeble body, nor the dread of
death, could arrest his gallant rush into
the forest of the battle. Oh! ye poor
patriots boys shrinking, dishonored men!

ye forget! *We are fighting for our country's liberty!* Look at him! and re-deem yourselves and your families from the inglorious past by a bold imitation of him in future, and we will gladly hail you as our noble brothers, our gallant compatriots in the purest, grandest cause on earth.

Ye multiplied thousands of *deserters*, hiding in the strongholds and dens of the mountains, or skulking about in the dark corners of the Confederacy; how mean ye feel! They who turn their backs upon such a cause, must, by all its exalted nobility, be crushed into the deepest degradation. From the very bottom of our hearts we pity you, our unhappy countrymen. What a stigma you have infixed upon your name! what a poison you have poured into your very hearts! On the day that you were mustered into the service, say, did you not swear that you would fight our country's battles to the end of the war? What

are you doing in the mountains? What
victories will you win there? What national independence will you establish
there? What respect and honor from
your fellow-men will you earn there?
What noble deeds to tell your children
will you achieve there? What brighten-
ing prospects for yourselves or your families, in time or eternity, do you expect
to light up by this shameless abandon-
ment of the sacred cause of your country and your race; the cause of all truth
and honor, of all justice and peace? Tell
me not of the inequalities of the Govern-
ment—of the oppression of your officers.
Be done with such trifling! Do you not
know that man is fallible; that, especially at such a time as this, there will be,
there must be some inequalities, some
improprieties? And have you no more
regard for your character, love for your
country, appreciation of the right, and
command of your intelligence than to
give up every great thing under heaven,

simply because every little thing about
you has not been done to your liking!
You are in the wrong, my countrymen,
grievously in the wrong. Come back to
the ranks, and come at once. Say! before high Heaven, did you not swear to
your comrades in arms that if they would
stand by you, you would stand by them?
that if they stood ready, in every fight,
to shoot down the man that aimed his
rifle at your breast, in every fight, by
their side you, too, would stand ready
to shoot down the men who aimed their
muskets at them? Alas! how many of
your faithful, noble comrades have been
slain in battle and sent to man's long
home, simply because you violated your
solemn oath and were not at your post
to defend them! Instead of destroying
our enemies, you have been strengthen-
ing them by the slaughter of your countrymen. Come back to the ranks, un-
faithful men! Look at our glorious
warrior! He might have saved his life

in the mountains and broken no pledge and violated no oath. Thank God! he needed none to make him faithful. He loved his country. He saw her peril. He fled to the rescue. He took your place. He shed his blood where, possibly, that very blood might have been spared had you but been half as faithful as he.— Come back to your country's standard; we need your plighted help; we will forget and forgive the past. We are going to triumph in this struggle; we will accord to you all the valor you exhibit, and share with you all the glory we shall win.

And oh! ye *valiant soldiers* who have stood your ground in every battle, and covered yourselves with glory in every conflict; who feel with us, that, God helping, you are going to struggle on to liberty or to death. We, who stand behind you, and are not permitted to fight by your side, for whom your breasts and hearts have been a shield in every ad-

vance of the enemy ; Oh! you know not
how we love, and honor, and prize you.
Believe us, whenever the tidings of your
gallant fighting reach our anxious ears,
we never fail to pour out our heartiest
love and gratitude to you, in the midst
of our solemn thanksgivings and praises
to God. Noble men! look ye, too, at
our sainted hero! See how the spirit of
your own breasts swelled in him! Like
you, he gave up everything for his country; like you, he faced every foe for his
country. Like him, gallant men, go
forth to the death for your country. Oh!
like him, let the love of God ever feed
your love of country; and, like him,
from your last battle field you will go
up to glory as in Elijah's chariot; and
while heaven opens wide her arms to
welcome you to your high home, earth
shall cheerfully enroll a *Christian* soldier
on the catalogue of her most splendid
noblemen.

II. Piety.—Yes, Capt. King loved his country. But if our soldier had not been a *pious* man, while we should have regretted this cardinal defect in his character as a *patriot*, we must have mourned without hope over the deadly lack in his character as a *man*. But thank God! though constitutionally bright and happy, he was a *consistent* Christian, and though uniformly modest and unostentatious, he was a *zealous* Christian.— From his youth he had been a professor of religion, in the Presbyterian church, and the war decidedly brightened the piety of his latter days. At the first prayer meeting he had the privilege of attending in his own sanctuary, after five months absence from it in the army, he stated to his brethren that the last words from his pastor, on leaving home, brought him this admonition: "Now, Tom, take care of your heart." With emotion he expressed to the congregation his trust in God, that he had not forgotten the seasonable exhortation—and surely the tenor of his life proved the truth of his protestation. -

The best practical test of a man's piety is his habitual treatment of the *Bible,* the *Mercy-seat,* and the Sabbath. In these three respects the aptitude of our soldier was conspicuous. From the day that he was mustered into the service until the day when he was compelled to leave it, in accordance with his original purpose, he regularly rose at four o'clock in the morning. The early and the closing hours of every day (Providence permitting) he conscientiously employed in scripture-reading and prayer. Surely *he* must have learned to pray, whose consciousness of this duty led him, a month at a time, to conduct family prayer regularly, both reading and praying, when disease had destroyed all power either to rise from his bed or to hold the Bible in his hand. And surely he must have learned to pray to edification, when another's servant confesses, on the Captain's death, that he had been accustomed to steal into his piazza by night, and kneel where he could hear most of the service through the closed door. Nor did he confine his Bible reading or his prayers to his tent; he was accustomed to read his Testament, solemnly and aloud, while marching—his Orderly reports—sometimes for consecutive miles. As for prayer, it was the admiring exclamation of his Lieutenant, "I never knew such a man; he was always praying!" We have equal evidence of his sensibility to the sacredness of the Sabbath. In his war-journal he makes the following records: "June 9th.—How war breaks in on the sanctity of this day! One has to keep a record of some kind or we lose all account of it. I hope when once we get into camp its sanctity will be observed." "June 15th.—We are promised a quiet Sabbath, and that our march shall not be renewed." He writes

to his wife—"Oh! how my heart was
gladdened by your letter to-day! How
different your quiet Sabbath from mine!
Mine was spent amidst the noise and
confusion of eighty men in miserable
box cars—the Sabbath of our arrival in
Knoxville—in unpacking the boys, and in
packing them up again for the night."—
In a subsequent letter he says, "Yester-
day, (Sabbath) much to my annoyance,
we had a muster for the pay-roll. I do
not see the necessity for this violation of
God's holy law, nor for the dress parade,
which is not omitted. Custom sanctions
it, but it makes the law of God of none
effect, and has a tendency to demoralize
the men, more or less; I wish it could
be done away with." Still later, he
writes to his brother that his brigade was
now on their march to the battle of Manassas. He felt deeply the responsibilities that awaited them. He longed in
spirit to be alone with God. In violation of his regular habit, at the break of

day, he left his tent and sought the quiet solitude of a neighboring grove. His soul waxed warm in prayer. The sun had shed no beams on earth when the serene, solemn Sabbath of universal nature was profanely broken by the roar of cannon at a distance. Then it was that his soul deeply rejoiced within him that this impious profanation of the sanctity of God's holy day was not perpetrated by Confederate troops; that though necessity was now laid upon *them*, and they, too, on God's holy Sabbath must handle these infernal destroyers of all quiet, peace and life, yet that the sin of all lay at the door of the enemy who had made the assault.

But Captain King's piety was not confined to personal fidelity in the use of the Bible, the Mercy-seat and the Sabbath; he ardently sought to *sanctify and to save men* by every means in his power—nor did he suffer any cross, however severe, to drive him from the path of duty. His men had left their religious privileges behind them; he felt that he should supply their destitution to the extent of his ability. Regularly, therefore, while he remained in the service, he summoned his company to family worship at his tent every evening. On these occasions he read the Scriptures, expounded and prayed. In his correspondence, he speaks of evening prayers at his marquee as "very pleasant to me, and well attended. God grant that His Spirit may move upon the hearts of our soldiers and much good be the result." He followed his public ministration with private effort. His soldiers testify that, at all convenient seasons, he was found earnestly conversing with his men upon the subject of personal religion; that he frequently accompanied an aged chaplain in his regimental visitations and, when the missionary's strength declined, spiritedly took up his work.

The actual reformation *of the men* is

another signal proof of the *zeal* of the officer. True! the captain's cheerful, abounding benevolence doubtless awakened no small part of the *idolatry* of his company; for what soldier could fail to love a captain who, not on duty, was as intimate with him as a brother, and watched over him with the affection and sympathy of a parent; who carried the soldier's musket and knapsack when weary, and fasted himself to feed his hungry private. But when a soldier's love for his captain *reforms* him, this fact establishes the *piety* of the officer, as well as his benevolence. It is pleasant to know that, in sympathy with our captain, no man of his company profaned God's holy name in his audience; and that to please him, the profanest waited cheerfully upon the evening service. "Boys! I never thought you would do this," was the kind but *serious* address of Captain King to the first few men of his company whom he had ever detected playing

cards. His Orderly sergeant testifies
that every card in camp was destroyed
that night, and not another handled until
the company had changed its captain,
adding that a large supply of marbles
was ingeniously substituted for the ban-
ished implements of gambling. Doubtless a number of similar moral and
religious impressions, convictions, and
reformations amongst the soldiers bear
testimony to the earnest piety of the
captain's personal example and public
and private addresses.

His uniform, earnest, and hopeful *ap-
peal to God under every heavy pressure,*
revealed his filial experience of God's
fidelity, and his consequent trust in God's
promises. When shot in the ankle at
Manassas, he stood up for some time on
one leg and held by the branch of a tree,
coolly giving orders, cheering on his men,
and praying aloud until it was necessary
that he should be removed. The moment
he found himself released from further

duty on the field, aware that he was leaving the battle undecided, he broke forth in the loudest strain of prayer that God would give victory to our army, and independence to the country. This supplication he continued while they carried him three hundred yards to the rear, and his soldiers say, for one hour and a half after he reached his resting place. It is a remarkable fact that, while passing through crowds of soldiers of different regiments, his loud prayer amazed and arrested a company of South Carolinians. At this juncture the wounded captain, espying a body of Zouaves not far distant, cried out to the Carolinians, " Forward boys !" The order they instantly and gallantly executed, capturing a portion, and driving the residue. A few days before his death, on the eve of his departure for Gen. Bragg's army, when his mother, wife, and children had received his solemn, tender adieu, in the parlor, and had followed him to the door,

their tears and words could scarcely
consent to his setting out upon so fearful
an enterprise in so much weakness. He
gently took them by the hand, led them
back to the family mercy-seat, and composed their disquietude by committing
himself and them to the guardianship of
God in such tender strains, with such
faltering accents as they will never forget.

Finally, *deliberate readiness for death
at all times*, sealed the sterling type of
his personal religion. He seemed to
keep death before him from the day of
his entering the army. He writes in his
war journal, "June 14.—We know that
many of us must fall martyrs in this
contest; but we do not doubt that we
have a father above who, knowing all
things, knows the justness of our cause—
and when He is for us, who can be against
us? On his way to Bragg army, he
was met by many of his friends who
earnestly pleaded with him to take no
part in the battle, alleging as a reason,

his imperfect command of his bodily powers. In substance he calmly replied, " It is my solemn conviction that, in the present emergency of the country, every man in Georgia who can reach the field should be found there. While so many remain at home, the least I can do is to represent the conviction of my soul by personal presence in the face of the enemy. If death does come, I trust I shall be ready for it." He was well aware of his danger. He announced to his body servant on taking leave of him, " You will never see my face again." Truly, he never did see his face again. Truly, when death advanced, he faced the King of terrors firmly. Mortally wounded, sensible that his end was rapidly approaching, his note book, pocket book, and the contents of his pockets, with perfect composure, he delivered to a bystanding officer, prescribing the disposition he would have made of them. He then solemnly avowed his belief in the Lord

Jesus Christ, and his perfect readiness to meet Him at his call; and thus, from a victorious battle-field, left us for the better land.

PATIOTISM AND PIETY! All we need in our country's emergency; the one brings us all the power of man, the other all the power of God. How eminently qualified was our departed soldier to serve his country, so decided both in his *piety* and in his *patriotism*.

My countrymen! God is the great *war maker*. "I bring the sword upon a land." God, the great *peace maker*. "He maketh peace." And war is God's *solemn arraignment of a people for national sin.* "In righteousness He judgeth and maketh war." This, OUR WAR, therefore, in the main, is—GOD ALMIGHTY, IN FATHERLY LOVE, DEALING WITH THE SOUTHERN CONFEDERACY FOR HER SIN.

Half angered, do you cry out, "Are not the *North* greater sinners than the *South*?" Grant it, what then? Does

this disprove the position? Did not
God frequently employ the heathen, by
war, to chastise Israel, and does not the
Bible say so? Was not Israel a better
people than the heathen, and does not
the Bible say so? Did not God take
greater interest in Israel than in the
heathen, and does not the Bible say so?
The very fact that Israel sinned, that
God loved Israel, and that he had purposed her sanctification in order to His
blessing—this it was—that constituted
the precise reason why God brought the
war of the heathen upon his people.
"Whom He loveth, He chasteneth, and
scourgeth every son whom He receiveth."
When God's word had failed, heathen
war was God's parental *rod*—speaking
loud to Israel, that she might be first
humbled and then blessed.   Look at our
country! not through northern character
nor any other false standard; look at
her through the *Bible*. To discern her
guilt one needs now no specification of

her most aggravated sins. Look at the whole *Confederate Church* of all names ! How far short she comes of that *world-converting work* required at her hand ! Look at the whole multitude of Confederate sinners of all classes ! How shamefully they neglect the great *God-fearing, soul-saving work* demanded of them ! If God's heart is set upon the world's conversion surely here is sin enough to kindle God's wrath and avert his blessing. Bear in mind, if heaven's blessing is ever to descend upon our country, there is no alternative, she must first be sanctified. His *word*, we can all testify, has been plentifully dispensed to us, but to little purpose. Therefore it is that he now resorts to the *rod*. Believe it my countrymen ! Oh, believe it ! *All these our sins, our personal, national sins, God in person, by this war, is charging home upon us.* And see ! if war is God's arraignment of a people for their sin— then *Southern sin* is *Federal power.*

For it is written, "Ye cannot stand before your enemies until ye put away the accursed thing." And *Southern humiliation* is *the utter rout of the North.* For thank God, whenever "Israel *cried* unto the Lord"—Yes! thank God! her enemy was always, instantly, gloriously *vanquished*, no matter what his power.

Oh! ye soldiers of the Confederate army! Our dear valued countrymen! know ye this—it is God's word to you— "When the host goeth forth against thine enemies, *then keep thee from every wicked thing.*" Tell me! for the victory of our arms, the overthrow of our enemies, our national independence, our personal liberties; for the cessation amongst us of all the horrors of intestine war; for the dispensation through all our borders of the blessings of a heaven-sent peace; and better, far better than all, for the promotion upon earth of human rectitude and divine salvation— will you not, my countrymen, will you

not put away all your profanities, all
your dishonesties, all your intemper-
ance, all your Sabbath breaking, all your
straggling, all your desertion? Will you
not give heed to the earnest voice of
your chaplains, and study the holy word
of God? Oh! for heaven and earth's
sake will you not rise up at once and
break off your sins by repentance, and
look to the Lord Jesus Christ for righteousness. Thank God for the augmented
religion of the army! But so many of
you have been left so far, far in the rear.
Oh! look before you at the noble example of your converted comrades, and
close up, close up on your file-leaders in
this march of national deliverance. We
especially commend unto you the character of our sainted captain. Like him,
forthwith cast in your mite of piety and
patriotism, and record this solemn reso-
lution—"As for me, if I fail in every other
work and object in life, I will go to the
grave and to the bar of God with the

happy consciousness that I have done
my part toward the deliverance of my
country in the day of her sore trial."
Noble soldiers! the Lord be with you!

Ye *cold Christians, formal professors,
and careless sinners* of the country!
You are working mightily to stregthen
Federal arms, to achieve Federal victories, and to crush the liberties of the
people. What deadly blows you daily
deal upon the property, honor, peace and
hope of the land. Oh, have mercy upon
us! Pity an oppresed nation struggling
for her very life. By your unrepented,
provoking transgressions, no longer draw
down the wrath of God upon our country. At last cast your mighty influence
upon the 'right side, and by an honest
return to God, put an end to this vile
war and light up the burdens that so
sorely oppress us.

And Oh, ye *avaricious, covetous, selfish men in all parts of the Confederacy,*
whose whole soul is absorbed in one con-

stant effort to improve this nick of time
and suck out of the weaknesses, perplex-
ities, and afflictions of disordered society, your own worldly prosperity! Alas!
cannot your sordid heart feel one solitary
pulsation of sympathy with all the woes
and perils of an injured, bleeding people?
Cannot your dark eye see that, under
the reign of benignant Omnipotence, in
your cherished idol you yourself are
building up a stupendous, an insufferable
curse? Are you entirely blind to the
frowns society knits upon you? Are
you utterly deaf to the scorn of all vir-
tuous minds crying out against you?—
Have you never marked how your griev-
ous selfishness, a stench in the nostrils
of Him who has said "Thou shalt love,"
is opening every vein of the nation, and
pouring out her very life-blood upon the
ground? Unhappy, guilty countrymen!
Awake from your deadly stupor and look
about you! Your shameful lack of patriotism and of piety is stirring up the

wrath of heaven, bringing on the Federal columns upon our soil, and cleaving down the struggling liberties of the people.— Do you wish to accomplish such a work as this? Oh, it is noble to love one's country, and nobler far to serve the God that made us. We beseech you, ponder well the portrait of our sainted soldier. Come now, and with all our fellow citizens throughout the length and breadth of our beloved Confederacy, we will go up and meet the enemy armed with *love of country and the love of God.* Ah, how soon shall the North be whipped into profound contrition for her most unrighteous and inhuman oppression of us! How soon shall the South become the freest, the happiest nation under heaven!

www.ingramcontent.com/pod-product-compliance
Lightning Source LLC
Chambersburg PA
CBHW021231260626
47172CB00002B/705